MW00915526

Interesting Facts For Smart Kids With Curious Minds

Challenging Activity Book For 8 Year Olds
In-Depth Facts About History, Science, Pop Culture, Holidays, Traveling, And More

By David W. Leon

Written by David W. Leon
Illustrated by Rhiannon Perrin

Table of Contents

Introduction

I grew up absorbed in fact books, I loved watching Jeopardy in the afternoons, and I signed up for way too many email subscriptions just to get their daily trivia email blasts. One thing I noticed with fact books lately is that the newer books seem to be falling flat, and upon further research, it seems I'm not the only person who has seen this unfortunate shift.

- Instead of being easy to read, now most fact books are overwhelmingly text intensive with minimal or no visuals.
- Instead of providing unique or obscure facts, now most trivia books regurgitate the same information.
- Instead of being age appropriate, now some fact books swing widely from appropriate facts to unexpectedly dark facts.

I've decided to try my hand at solving the above issues and created a new way to engage with the trivia!

If you're like me and love to have fun while learning about crazy and quirky facts, then I might just have the solution for you. I hope you enjoy!

Level 1
Fun Fact Frenzy

Questions 1-20

Flex Your Brain And Learn Something New!

Interesting Facts For Smart Kids
With Curious Minds

Question 1

Which ancient civilization did Socrates, Plato, and Aristotle belong to?

a) Roman

b) Egyptian

c) Greek

d) Spanish

David W. Leon
Fun Facts Books

Answer 1

Socrates, Plato, and Aristotle were philosophers who lived in ancient Greece during the Hellenistic period. The city of Athens received taxes from the rest of the polis and lived a golden era. It allowed the development of theater, philosophy, and democracy as the political system.

Interesting Facts For Smart Kids
With Curious Minds

Question 2

In what Florida attraction will you see the Space Shuttle Atlantis and have the opportunity to experience what it feels like when a Space Shuttle is launched?

a) Kennedy Space Center

b) Disneyland

c) City Walk

d) Universal Studios

David W. Leon
Fun Facts Books

Answer 2

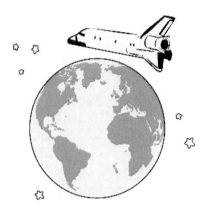

Located on Merritt Island, Florida, The Kennedy Space Center has Mission Zones that allow visitors to experience the history of NASA and space exploration. The Center is the permanent home of the Space Shuttle Atlantis, which is surrounded by more than sixty exhibits that highlight the importance of the space shuttle to space exploration history.

Interesting Facts For Smart Kids
With Curious Minds

Question 3

Why do we put salt on sidewalks when it snows?

a) Salt summons the magical snow-dissolving fairies

b) Salt automatically dissolves

c) Salt lowers the freezing point of pure water

d) We don't put salt on snowy sidewalks

David W. Leon
Fun Facts Books

Answer 3

Salt lowers the freezing point of water, causing it to melt and preventing the formation of ice. It also provides better traction, making it safer for pedestrians and vehicles to navigate icy surfaces.

Interesting Facts For Smart Kids
With Curious Minds

Question 4

What is the name of the New York City store that hosts the Thanksgiving Day parade each year?

a) JCPenney

b) Macy's

c) Best Buy

d) Target

Answer 4

Since 1924, the Macy's Department Store has hosted New York City's famous Thanksgiving Day parade. The parade usually features huge balloons of beloved cartoon figures like Snoopy, Papa Smurf, and Bart Simpson.

Interesting Facts For Smart Kids
With Curious Minds

Question 5

How did Harriet Tubman help enslaved people in the 19th century?

a) "Conducted" the Underground Railroad

b) Was a soldier of the Confederation

c) Organized a mutiny

d) Set fire to her master's crops

David W. Leon
Fun Facts Books

Answer 5

Harriet Tubman was an enslaved woman who escaped and then helped other people to escape through the Underground Railroad. She was also a soldier in the Union Army, a nurse, and a spy. Although there was a prize for her life, she was never caught.

Interesting Facts For Smart Kids
With Curious Minds

Question 6

What Christian church in Turkey is known for its stunning architecture and colorful mosaics?

a) Canterbury Cathedral

b) Hagia Sophia

c) St. John's Abbey

d) St. Paul's Cathedral

Answer 6

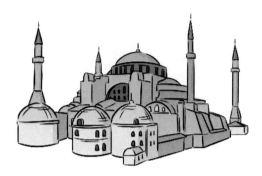

Built during the 6th century, The Church of the Holy Wisdom, commonly known as the Hagia Sophia, is one of the most famous churches in the world. The church features an unusual design consisting of a unique longitudinal basilica and a 105-foot dome. The mosaics of the Hagia Sophia feature the Virgin Mary and depictions of the saints.

Interesting Facts For Smart Kids
With Curious Minds

Question 7

The thought experiment known as Schrödinger's cat postulates that a cat can be in two states at the same time. What are those two states?

a) Alive and dead

b) Moving and stationary

c) Adult and kitten

d) Awake and asleep

Answer 7

Schrödinger's cat is a thought experiment proposed by physicist Erwin Schrödinger to illustrate the peculiarities of quantum mechanics. It suggests that a cat in a closed box can be both alive and dead at the same time until observed, illustrating the peculiarities of quantum superposition and the role of observation in determining reality.

Interesting Facts For Smart Kids
With Curious Minds

Question 8

What bird is often found on the Thanksgiving table in the United States?

a) Chicken

b) Rooster

c) Turkey

d) Pheasant

Answer 8

While historians aren't sure what fowl was served at the first Thanksgiving, the turkey has become a staple of the holiday table. Some historians have suggested that the turkey became the popular meal of choice because it is a large bird capable of feeding a large family.

Interesting Facts For Smart Kids
With Curious Minds

Question 9

In the 7th century, a new empire spread over the north of Africa and reached Spain and Portugal. Who were the people of the new empire?

a) Romans

b) Vikings

c) Macedonians

d) Arabs

Answer 9

Soon after Islam's founder, Prophet Muhammad, died, his heirs decided to spread their faith. They left the Arabian Peninsula and conquered lands in Asia and all the northern part of Africa. Later, they conquered almost all of the Iberian Peninsula. They intended to expand into Europe but the Frenchman Charles Martel stopped them.

Interesting Facts For Smart Kids
With Curious Minds

Question 10

What Australian beach has iceberg pools and a licensed surf school?

a) Manly Beach

b) Squeaky Beach

c) Bondi Beach

d) Mermaid Beach

Answer 10

Located in Sydney, Australia, Bondi Beach is one of Australia's most iconic beaches. Bondi Beach is a popular place for surfers and has a licensed surfer school for those who want to learn how to ride the waves. It also has famous sapphire pools known as the Bondi Icebergs.

Interesting Facts For Smart Kids
With Curious Minds

Question 11

What color is not found in a rainbow?

a) Black

b) Red

c) Green

d) Violet

David W. Leon
Fun Facts Books

Answer 11

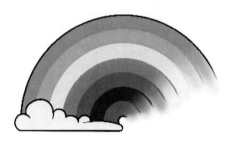

Scientists use the acronym ROYGBIV (pronounced Roy G. Biv) to recite the seven colors in a rainbow: red, orange, yellow, green, blue, indigo, and violet. Black is not a color that would be visible in a rainbow.

Interesting Facts For Smart Kids
With Curious Minds

Question 12

What family member should you celebrate on April 10th each year?

a) Uncle

b) Mom

c) Sibling

d) Grandfather

Answer 12

Created by Claudia Evart in 1995 after the deaths of her brother and sister, National Siblings Day is a day reserved for celebrating your brother or sister. Three presidents have officially recognized this event, and there is a Siblings Day Foundation that is encouraging the United Nations to recognize this day as a worldwide event.

Interesting Facts For Smart Kids
With Curious Minds

Question 13

When did most African countries begin their independence processes?

a) In the Middle Ages

b) In ancient times

c) In the 20th century

d) In the 21st century

David W. Leon
Fun Facts Books

Answer 13

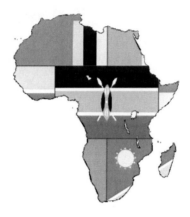

Most of the current African countries gained their independence in the 20th century. Before that, the territories were European powers' colonies. Apart from the ancient empires, the continent was occupied and divided by European countries between the 15th and 19th centuries.

Interesting Facts For Smart Kids
With Curious Minds

Question 14

What bird native to New Zealand is considered a national icon that should be protected because of its vulnerability to predators?

a) Pelican

b) Kiwi

c) Seagull

d) Pigeon

Answer 14

With their underdeveloped wings and lack of sternum, the Kiwi is vulnerable to predators like cats and dogs. There are approximately ninety groups in New Zealand trying to protect and preserve the bird that has become a national symbol.

Interesting Facts For Smart Kids
With Curious Minds

Question 15

Which animals are also known as "sea cows?"

a) Dolphins

b) Manatees

c) Whales

d) Walruses

Answer 15

Sea cows, also known as manatees, are large marine mammals that inhabit warm, shallow coastal waters and rivers. There are three living species of sea cows: the West Indian manatee, the Amazonian manatee, and the African manatee.

Interesting Facts For Smart Kids
With Curious Minds

Question 16

What object with the nickname "Old Glory" is celebrated on June 14th in the United States?

a) Flag

b) Broom

c) Cannon

d) Ship

Answer 16

While the American flag has changed its design several times, Flag Day is a holiday that celebrates the history of "Old Glory." The stripes on the flag represent the thirteen original colonies while the stars represent each of the fifty states.

Interesting Facts For Smart Kids
With Curious Minds

Question 17

Before the revolution in 1917, Russia was an empire and was ruled by a tsar. Who was the last Russian Tsar?

a) Mikjail Gorbachov

b) Charles De Gaulle

c) Nicolai Románov

d) Ivan IV the Terrible

Answer 17

The word "tsar" means king and the last tsar of the Russian Empire was Nicolai Románov. The Russian Revolution began in 1917 while the country was involved in World War I. The situation for the Russian population had turned unbearable.

Interesting Facts For Smart Kids
With Curious Minds

Question 18

What is the name of the Turkish bazaar with over sixty-one covered streets that attracts millions of visitors from around the world each year?

a) Grand Bazaar

b) Izmailovsky Market

c) The Witches' Market

d) Central Market

David W. Leon
Fun Facts Books

Answer 18

Now considered one of the first shopping malls in the world, The Grand Bazaar in Istanbul has over four thousand shops and anywhere from 200,000 to 450,000 visitors daily. The Grand Bazaar was first launched between 1455-1456 to stimulate the economy of Turkey. Over the years, it has grown to employ approximately twenty-five thousand people daily.

Interesting Facts For Smart Kids
With Curious Minds

Question 19

What is a particle smaller than an atom called?

a) Subatomic Particle

b) Standard Model

c) Magnetic Field

d) Antimatter

Answer 19

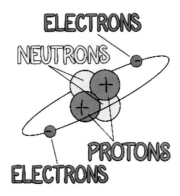

Self-contained units of energy or matter are called subatomic particles, also known as elementary particles. Protons, electrons, and neutrons are all considered subatomic particles because they cannot be broken down into smaller units.

Interesting Facts For Smart Kids
With Curious Minds

Question 20

What James Joyce novel is celebrated with the Irish holiday Bloomsday?

a) A Portrait of the Artist as a Young Man

b) Dubliners

c) Finnegan's Wake

d) Ulysses

Answer 20

Every June 16th, the city of Dublin celebrates Joyce's 265,000 word tome entitled Ulysses. Participants wear bowler hats and enjoy a plethora of performances, re-enactments, and readings of the James Joyce masterpiece.

Level 2
Smart Challenges

Questions 21-40

Acing The Quiz So Far?

Let's See If You Can Keep Your Momentum!

Interesting Facts For Smart Kids
With Curious Minds

Question 21

What was Albert Einstein's most transcendent contribution to science?

a) Theory of relativity

b) Black holes theory

c) Uncertainty principle

d) Heliocentric theory

Answer 21

The German scientist Albert Einstein made significant contributions to science, explaining the behavior and composition of light and the relation between mass and energy among others. But he is most renowned for his general theory of relativity.

Interesting Facts For Smart Kids
With Curious Minds

Question 22

How many steps will you climb altogether at the Paris Catacombs?

a) 131

b) 243

c) 112

d) 300

David W. Leon
Fun Facts Books

Answer 22

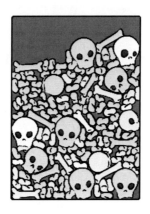

The Paris Catacombs, which has the depth of a five-story building, has 131 steps going down and 112 steps to climb back up, equaling 243 steps altogether. The catacombs were created in the 17th century when the cemeteries of Paris were moved underground due to health concerns. It now takes about an hour to walk the length of the catacombs, where bones and skulls are carefully organized and displayed.

Interesting Facts For Smart Kids
With Curious Minds

Question 23

How many bones do sharks have?

a) 100

b) 2

c) 0

d) 25

Answer 23

Sharks, like other fish, have a skeletal structure made up of cartilage rather than bones. Cartilage is a flexible and lightweight material that provides support and structure to their bodies. It is different from the hard bones found in most vertebrate animals.

Interesting Facts For Smart Kids
With Curious Minds

Question 24

What holiday celebrates pale skin people who wear black and listen to dark and moody music?

a) World Goth Day

b) Loomis Day

c) International Tiara Day

d) Culture Freedom Day

Answer 24

Celebrating the gloomy subculture that developed in Great Britain in the 1970s, World Goth Day celebrates those who wear black a lot and enjoy music with darker themes. Although Goths have sometimes been given a bad rap, World Goth Day was officially created by the DJs of a highly successful BBC radio program that celebrated the music genre. On May 22nd each year you can celebrate the holiday by listening to some gothic music, going to a concert, or attending a charity event.

Interesting Facts For Smart Kids
With Curious Minds

Question 25

What was the name of the empire that unified all the tribes in the central steppes of Asia in the 13th century?

a) The Huns

b) The Mongols

c) The Macedonians

d) The Babylonians

Answer 25

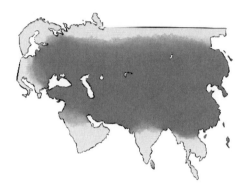

The Mongol Empire dominated the Asian steppes from the Pacific coast of Asia to the margins of the Danube River in Europe. There is no solid evidence of the origins of these nomadic tribes that were able to build the greatest empire in history.

Interesting Facts For Smart Kids
With Curious Minds

Question 26

Where in Asheville, North Carolina, is the Antler Hill Village & Winery?

a) Thomas Wolfe's Home

b) The Biltmore Estate

c) Asheville Urban Trail

d) Basilica of Saint Lawrence

Answer 26

The country home that George Vanderbilt built in 1895 is now known as the Biltmore Estate. The 8,000-acre property is not only home to the Antler Hill Village and Winery but also includes an inn, an equestrian center, and numerous restaurants.

Interesting Facts For Smart Kids
With Curious Minds

Question 27

Who is known as the father of psychoanalysis?

a) Sigmund Freud

b) Carl Rogers

c) Ivan Pavlov

d) Carl Sagan

Answer 27

Sigmund Freud was an Austrian neurologist and psychologist who developed the field of psychoanalysis, a clinical method for treating psychological disorders and understanding the human mind. He introduced concepts such as the unconscious mind, the interpretation of dreams, and the role of the unconscious in shaping behavior and personality.

Interesting Facts For Smart Kids
With Curious Minds

Question 28

What day would be a good time to read a five-line poem meant to make you laugh?

a) National Haiku Day

b) Mother Goose Day

c) National Limerick Day

d) Caldecott Day

David W. Leon
Fun Facts Books

Answer 28

Celebrated on Edward Lear's birthday, who wrote a book of limericks called A Book of Nonsense, National Limerick Day is May 12th. Limericks are intended to be funny poems consisting of five-lines and an AABBA rhyming style.

Interesting Facts For Smart Kids
With Curious Minds

Question 29

Who was the warrior and leader of the nomadic tribe that conquered the territories in southern Asia from the Tibet steppe to the Adriatic Sea?

a) Attila the Hun

b) Qin Shi Huang

c) Cyrus the Great

d) Genghis Khan

Answer 29

The Mongol Empire was ruled by the warrior king Genghis Khan. He unified all the Mongol tribes that were scattered throughout the Asian steppes at the beginning of the 13th century. The Mongol people consolidated as a confederation, and Khan conquered lands on two continents.

Interesting Facts For Smart Kids
With Curious Minds

Question 30

In what part of Germany is the town of Baden-Baden, which has a mineral water bathing temple?

a) Bavaria

b) Lower Saxony

c) Black Forest

d) Schleswig-Holstein

Answer 30

The traditional Irish spa Friedrichsbad Roman-Irish Bath is one of thirty spas located in the Black Forest town of Baden-Baden. When the Romans arrived in the Black Forest, a 100-mile stretch of dense forest, they brought the practice of communal bathing with them. The spas in Baden-Baden are an offshoot of that history.

Interesting Facts For Smart Kids
With Curious Minds

Question 31

Which of these metals can you melt in your hands?

a) Zinc

b) Plutonium

c) Silver

d) Gallium

Answer 31

Similar to aluminum, gallium is a soft, silvery-white metal that can melt in the warmth of your hands. Gallium melts at 85.6°F, but boils at 4044°F, making it a useful metal for measuring temperatures that would melt an ordinary thermometer.

Interesting Facts For Smart Kids
With Curious Minds

Question 32

What item does Douglas Adams claim "is about the most massively useful thing an interstellar hitchhiker can have?"

a) Flashlight

b) Shovel

c) Fork

d) Towel

Answer 32

Adams' novel The Hitchhiker's Guide to the Galaxy spawned Towel Day, a holiday for Adams' fans held on May 25th each year. Fans of Adams' book series carry a towel with them all day like Arthur Kent, the main character in the books.

Interesting Facts For Smart Kids
With Curious Minds

Question 33

In 1986, there was an important incident at a nuclear power station in the Soviet Union. In which city was that station located?

a) Moscow

b) Chernobyl

c) Pryp'yat

d) Kyiv

David W. Leon
Fun Facts Books

Answer 33

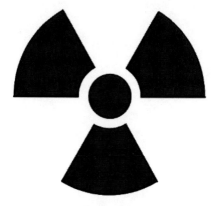

A nuclear accident happened in the city of Chernobyl. A defective nuclear reactor was mistakenly manipulated by the operators, which caused an explosion and a fire in the nuclear station. Besides the casualties from the explosion and fire, the station continued to radiate radioactivity.

Interesting Facts For Smart Kids
With Curious Minds

Question 34

What do the aboriginal people of Australia call Ayers Rock, which they view as a sacred landmark?

a) Mena Creek

b) Denham

c) New South Wales Shark Bay

d) Uluru

David W. Leon
Fun Facts Books

Answer 34

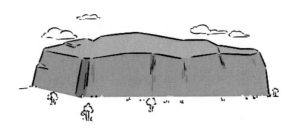

Ayers Rock, which the Aborigines call Uluru Rock, is the largest monolith on Earth. The rock, known for its stunning fiery, orange-red color, is made of sandstone and feldspar.

Interesting Facts For Smart Kids
With Curious Minds

Question 35

What would happen to a glass of water in space?

a) It would freeze

b) It would boil

c) It would stay the same

d) It would glow

Answer 35

Since space is a vacuum, water would boil because it boils in any kind of vacuum. Once the water boils, it could vaporize into ice cubes or remain a gas, depending on whether it was in the sunlight, floating in darkness, or in contact with another substance.

Interesting Facts For Smart Kids
With Curious Minds

Question 36

Whose birthday should you celebrate by wearing a cardigan, feeding the fish, and having a beautiful day in your neighborhood?

a) Tom Hanks

b) Roald Dahl

c) Fred Rogers

d) Mother Goose

David W. Leon
Fun Facts Books

Answer 36

March 20th, the birthday of Mr. Fred Rogers, is Won't You Be My Neighbor Day. The holiday celebrates the beloved host of "Mr. Roger's Neighborhood," a popular children's program during the 1970s and 1980s. Mr. Rogers always started the show by coming home, putting on his cardigan, and feeding the fish.

Interesting Facts For Smart Kids
With Curious Minds

Question 37

In which current country was that nuclear power station located?

a) The Soviet Union

b) Belarus

c) Lithuania

d) Ukraine

Answer 37

Chernobyl is located in current Ukraine. In 1986, it was still part of the USSR. In 1991, the Soviet Union began a process of disintegration and the former republics declared their independence. From then on, Ukraine became a sovereign state.

Interesting Facts For Smart Kids
With Curious Minds

Question 38

How tall is Chicago's Sears Tower?

a) 1454 feet

b) 2000 feet

c) 100 feet

d) 1800 feet

Answer 38

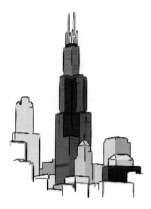

Once the world's tallest building, the Sears Tower has 110 stories and is 1454 feet tall. Although other buildings have surpassed its height, the Sears Tower still has the highest roof deck and elevator ride.

Interesting Facts For Smart Kids
With Curious Minds

Question 39

Slugs and snails are less commonly known as what?

a) Gastropods

b) Cephalopods

c) Arthropods

d) Cetaceans

Answer 39

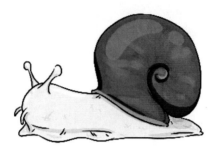

Slugs and snails are less commonly known as gastropods. Both slugs and snails are part of the same biological group, and gastropod refers to the way they glide on a muscular structure on their underside.

Interesting Facts For Smart Kids
With Curious Minds

Question 40

International Children's Book Day is celebrated on which author's birthday?

a) Judy Blume

b) Mo Willems

c) Lewis Carroll

d) Hans Christian Anderson

Answer 40

Since 1967, International Children's Book Day has been celebrated on April 2nd, which is the birthday of Hans Christian Anderson. Anderson was a Danish children's author who became famous for his fairy tales like "The Princess and the Pea" and "The Snow Queen."

You're almost halfway through!

If you've made it this far, I assume you are a true smartie who is willing to learn new things.

Remember, it is totally fine to not get every question right. This game is designed to stretch your mind and teach you new facts from around the world and throughout time!

If you have 2 minutes before the next level, providing feedback will greatly help me for writing future books and will also help other readers when looking at this book.

What do you think of the book so far?

Open the camera app on your phone
Hold phone so the QR Code appears in view
Tap the pop-up link for the QR Code

Level 3
Discover The World's Mysteries

Questions 41-60

The World Is Full Of Wonders!

Have You Discovered Something New About Another Culture?

Interesting Facts For Smart Kids
With Curious Minds

Question 41

The capital of the Byzantine Empire was Constantinople, which still exists under a different name. What is that city called today?

a) N'Khara

b) Athens

c) Istanbul

d) Damascus

Answer 41

Istanbul was founded by the Roman Emperor Constantine the Great and initially named Constantinople after him. It used to be the capital city of Byzantium and the Ottoman Empire. The capital of the current Republic of Turkey, the modern country made up of ancient Byzantine territories, is Ankara.

Interesting Facts For Smart Kids
With Curious Minds

Question 42

Where in New Zealand can you have a beer at the Green Dragon Inn?

a) Abel Tasman National Park

b) The Hobbiton Movie Set

c) Queenstown

d) Rotorua

Answer 42

After visiting some of the sites where the Lord of the Ring movies were filmed, visitors of Hobbiton, Matamata, can end their tour with a beer at the inn. A two-hour tour will take you through the Shire and the tiny houses the Hobbits lived in.

Interesting Facts For Smart Kids
With Curious Minds

Question 43

Why are snowflakes always six-sided?

a) The molecular structure of water forms them that way

b) They form that way in the clouds

c) They're not always six-sided

d) They form that way when they land

David W. Leon
Fun Facts Books

Answer 43

Snowflakes are always six-sided because of the way water molecules arrange themselves when they freeze. Water molecules are made up of two hydrogen atoms and one oxygen atom, and they naturally form a triangular shape. When water freezes, these molecules join in a repeating pattern, and the most stable arrangement is a hexagonal shape.

Interesting Facts For Smart Kids
With Curious Minds

Question 44

What day is a public holiday in twenty states and marks the beginning of the Christmas shopping season?

a) Cyber Monday

b) Christmas Eve

c) Black Friday

d) Giving Tuesday

Answer 44

Even in states that don't recognize Black Friday as a public holiday, the day after Thanksgiving is recognized as the start of the Christmas shopping season. Black Friday is the day that stores offer deep discounts and is usually one of the busiest shopping days of the entire year.

Interesting Facts For Smart Kids
With Curious Minds

Question 45

Charlie Chaplin left a footprint in the history of cinema. What characterized his filmography?

a) Color

b) Absence of music

c) Silence

d) Single actor

Answer 45

Charlie Chaplin was the master of pantomime and starred in many comedies, all filmed in black and white and without dialogue. He is an icon in silent films. Modern Times and The Great Dictator are some of his greatest movies.

Interesting Facts For Smart Kids
With Curious Minds

Question 46

Which Canadian garden has a Sunken Garden, a Mediterranean Garden, and a Rose Garden?

a) The Butchart Gardens

b) Edwardian Gardens at Government House

c) Montréal Botanical Garden

d) Kingsbrae Garden

Answer 46

Now named after the garden's creator Victoria Butchart, The Butchart Gardens in Victoria, British Columbia, attracts a million visitors a year. In 2004, on the 100th anniversary of the creation of the gardens, Butchart Garden was declared a national historic site of Canada.

Interesting Facts For Smart Kids
With Curious Minds

Question 47

What does a person suffering from pronoia mistakenly believe?

a) That everyone is against them

b) That they are going to die

c) That everyone is on their side

d) That they are the funniest person in the room

Answer 47

Sometimes called "reverse paranoia," a person with pronoia mistakenly believes that others are conspiring to help them. Unlike paranoia, which involves unfounded beliefs of persecution or harm, pronoia involves unfounded beliefs of support, assistance, and positive intentions from others.

Interesting Facts For Smart Kids
With Curious Minds

Question 48

What do Muslims do during the month of Ramadan in addition to prayer and faithful intention?

a) Fast

b) Gift Giving

c) Cooking

d) Writing

Answer 48

Fasting during the month of Ramadan is considered one of the Five Pillars of Islam, and Muslims believe that God will forgive sins during this month of restraint and prayer. In the Muslim calendar, which is shorter than the Gregorian calendar, Ramadan begins and ends with a crescent moon.

Interesting Facts For Smart Kids
With Curious Minds

Question 49

What is the Hammurabi Code?

a) An Egyptian papyrus

b) A Babylonian manuscript

c) A Persian song

d) What is written on the Rosetta Stone

David W. Leon
Fun Facts Books

Answer 49

The Hammurabi Code is a manuscript written in the 2nd millennium B.C.E. under Hammurabi's reign. He ruled the Babylonian Empire in Asian Mesopotamia. It contains 282 laws, one of them being the famous "an eye for an eye".

Interesting Facts For Smart Kids
With Curious Minds

Question 50

What is the name of the tulip farm in Holland that welcomes nearly a million visitors a year?

a) Holland Ridge Farms

b) Wooden Shoe Tulip Farm

c) Dutch Hollow Farms

d) Keukenhof Tulip Garden

David W. Leon
Fun Facts Books

Answer 50

Open from March 23rd to May 14th in the city of Lisse, the tulip garden has a walking 15-kilometer (9 miles) walking path. Keukenhof Gardens opened in 1950 and has hosted up to forty growers each year.

Interesting Facts For Smart Kids
With Curious Minds

Question 51

What process does the term "Spaghettification" describe?

a) What happens to matter that gets too close to a black hole

b) The strange debris found on Mars

c) The building of spacecraft with spaghetti

d) Describes the explosion of a gamma ray burst

Answer 51

Spaghettification is a real term that describes what happens when matter gets too close to a black hole and gets squeezed horizontally and stretched vertically. This is sometimes called the "noodle effect" because matter ends up looking like strings of spaghetti.

Interesting Facts For Smart Kids
With Curious Minds

Question 52

If you're from New Jersey, what is the day before Halloween called?

a) The Day Before Halloween

b) Samhain

c) Mischief Night

d) All Souls Day

Answer 52

Starting in the late 1950s, New Jersey teens would get together for a night of pranks called Mischief Night. On the night before Halloween, firecrackers, using toilet paper to decorate someone's yard, and exploding pumpkins were some of the typical pranks. The tradition also extends to Cincinnati (where it's called "Cabbage Night") and Detroit (where it's known as "Devil's Night").

Interesting Facts For Smart Kids
With Curious Minds

Question 53

Which of the following monuments is considered one of the seven wonders of the ancient world?

a) The Statue of Liberty

b) The Great Wall of China

c) The Lighthouse of Alexandria

d) The Eiffel Tower

Answer 53

The seven wonders of the ancient world were created by ancient civilizations. The Lighthouse of Alexandria was one of them. Placed on the small island of Pharos, in Alexandria, it was built by the Macedonians after they conquered Egypt in the 3rd century B.C.E.

Interesting Facts For Smart Kids
With Curious Minds

Question 54

Where is the 555-foot marble obelisk built to honor George Washington?

a) New York City

b) Atlanta, Georgia

c) Richmond, Virginia

d) Washington, D.C.

David W. Leon
Fun Facts Books

Answer 54

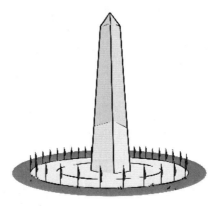

Towering over Washington D.C., the Washington Monument is an iconic attraction in the United States capital city. The monument opened to the public on October 8, 1888.

Interesting Facts For Smart Kids
With Curious Minds

Question 55

What is the loudest animal on Earth?

a) Elephant

b) Spider Monkey

c) Tiger

d) Sperm Whale

Answer 55

Sperm whales are known for producing the loudest sound of any animal, both above and below the water. The clicks produced by sperm whales can exceed 230 decibels (dB) underwater, which is much louder than a jet engine. However, some scientists believe that blue whales are as loud or louder than sperm whales because of how long they can make a single sound.

Interesting Facts For Smart Kids
With Curious Minds

Question 56

If you are a music lover, what holiday in April is probably marked on your calendar?

a) Hug a Musician Day

b) Mariachi Day

c) National DJ Day

d) Record Store Day

Answer 56

Initially started to celebrate independently owned record stores, since 2008 Record Store Day has become one of the busiest shopping days for music lovers. "RSD Releases" are released in limited quantities on one Saturday every April (the date changes every year). Record Store Day is now celebrated on every continent except Antarctica.

Interesting Facts For Smart Kids
With Curious Minds

Question 57

What political system did Rome have before becoming an empire?

a) A monarchy

b) A republic

c) A democracy

d) A feudal system

Answer 57

Before Julius Caesar concentrated all the power and laid the foundations for the empire, Rome was a republic. Apart from the individual governors, such as the Dictator or the Consul, there were institutions where the people could participate—such as the Senate for the patricians, and the popular Assemblies for the plebeians, or common people.

Interesting Facts For Smart Kids
With Curious Minds

Question 58

Where would you travel in China to see hundreds of life-size terracotta soldiers, horses, and chariots in battle array?

a) Beijing

b) Shanghai

c) Xi'an

d) Kunming

Answer 58

The Terracotta Army in Xi'an, China, is officially known as The Qin Tomb Terracotta Warriors and Horses. Now considered one of the great archeological finds of the 20th century, the Terracotta Army was found in the tomb of China's First Emperor. The tomb was constructed by 720,000 people and took about forty years to build.

Interesting Facts For Smart Kids
With Curious Minds

Question 59

What kind of material do spiders spin to make their webs?

a) Cotton

b) Silk

c) Taffeta

d) Polyester

David W. Leon
Fun Facts Books

Answer 59

Spiders have organs called spinnerets which spin out a silk that is stronger than any man-made material on Earth. Despite its strength, spider silk is remarkably lightweight and pliable: it can be stretched to 140% of its length without breaking.

Interesting Facts For Smart Kids
With Curious Minds

Question 60

What kind of music is celebrated with a holiday on January 21st in Mexico?

a) Tango Day

b) Mariachi Day

c) Polka Day

d) Waltz Day

Answer 60

Native to Western Mexico, mariachi music is a blending of traditional music and foreign musical influences. Mariachi bands have been around since 1852 and have become a symbol of national pride in Mexico.

Level 4

Who's The Brightest Bulb In Your Family?

Questions 61-80

Try Putting Your Family To The Test And See Who Gets The Most Questions In This Next Level!

Interesting Facts For Smart Kids
With Curious Minds

Question 61

What was feudalism?

a) Lands conquered by the Romans

b) A synonym for absolute monarchy

c) Social, economic, & political organization

d) The first empires in ancient times

David W. Leon
Fun Facts Books

Answer 61

Feudalism was the social, economic, and political organization of western European societies during the Middle Ages. The fiefs were lands ruled by the manor lords, who could only be nobles or clerics. The serfs were allowed to live on their land as long as they paid for that right with work.

Interesting Facts For Smart Kids
With Curious Minds

Question 62

What sea is 423 meters below sea level, making it the lowest point on Earth?

a) The Dead Sea

b) Arabian Sea

c) Caribbean Sea

d) Aegean Sea

Answer 62

Bordering both Israel and Jordan, The Dead Sea, sometimes called The Salt Sea, is not swimmable because of the high salt content in the water. However, many visitors float in the Dead Sea, which many believe has therapeutic and healing qualities. There is so much salt in The Dead Sea that visitors don't have to do anything because the water buoys them up.

Interesting Facts For Smart Kids
With Curious Minds

Question 63

There are six universal facial expressions: anger, disgust, fear, happiness, and sadness are five of them. What is the sixth?

a) Confusion

b) Surprise

c) Joy

d) Consternation

Answer 63

Surprise is considered one of the core universal emotions expressed through facial expressions. It is characterized by widened eyes, raised eyebrows, an open mouth, and an overall facial expression of astonishment or sudden realization. Some scientists believe that contempt should be added as a seventh universal facial expression, but the debate is ongoing.

Interesting Facts For Smart Kids
With Curious Minds

Question 64

What are people encouraged to do on Martin Luther King Day?

a) Pray

b) Volunteer

c) Travel

d) Work

Answer 64

On the third Monday of January, Americans are encouraged to volunteer in their communities on Martin Luther King Day. The holiday honors the civil rights leader who gave the famous "I Have a Dream" speech in Washington, D.C., in 1963.

Interesting Facts For Smart Kids
With Curious Minds

Question 65

What was the main economic activity during feudalism?

a) Commerce

b) Agriculture

c) Industrial manufacturing

d) All of the above

Answer 65

The main activity during feudalism was agriculture. Although commerce was very intense in ancient times, it declined after the fall of the Roman Empire. Money had almost disappeared. The times were turbulent, and roads were dangerous for merchants.

Interesting Facts For Smart Kids
With Curious Minds

Question 66

In what Chicago park is the Cloud Gate landmark?

a) Millennium Park

b) Lincoln Park

c) Jackson Park

d) Humboldt Park

Answer 66

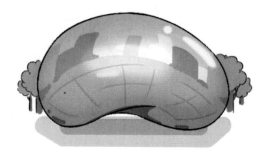

While Chicagoans refer to the reflecting sculpture as "The Bean," Cloud Gate has become one of the most popular features of Millennium Park. Cloud Gate serves as an entrance to the park, and its surface reflects the visitors' as well as the city skyline.

Interesting Facts For Smart Kids
With Curious Minds

Question 67

When someone has body odor, what is causing the bad smell?

a) Bacteria

b) Sweat

c) Hair Follicles

d) Eccrine Glands

Answer 67

Sweat itself is generally odorless, but when it comes into contact with bacteria on the skin's surface, particularly in areas with high concentrations of sweat glands like the armpits or feet, it can create an unpleasant smell. The bacteria metabolize the sweat, producing volatile compounds that result in body odor.

Interesting Facts For Smart Kids
With Curious Minds

Question 68

Why was the Roman festival of Parentalia celebrated for a week each February?

a) To Honor Family Ancestors

b) New Year's Celebrations

c) To Have Feasts

d) Dancing and the Consumption of Wine

Answer 68

While the Romans are known for their many wild and energetic festivals, Parentalia was a quiet time for families to gather and honor their dead. Throughout the week, families would perform private rituals for the deceased, sometimes leaving offerings of bread and wine. At the end of the week, the community would gather for a larger festival to honor the dead.

Interesting Facts For Smart Kids
With Curious Minds

Question 69

What was the economic plan implemented by President F.D. Roosevelt to reverse the effects of the Great Depression?

a) The Marshall Plan

b) The New Deal

c) Stability and Growth Pact

d) The Rebuilding Plan

Answer 69

The Great Depression made the global market collapse, and the principles of the capitalist system were questioned. The market had failed to guarantee stability and wealth. Then, President Roosevelt proposed a plan called the New Deal. It involved more intervention of the state in the economy.

Interesting Facts For Smart Kids
With Curious Minds

Question 70

What is the name of the 4100-mile river in Africa that flows from south to north?

a) Limpopo River

b) Yellow River

c) Congo River

d) Nile River

Answer 70

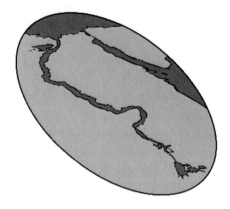

Critical to the development of Ancient Egypt, the Nile River is the longest river in the world. It is also the only river that flows backward and runs along or through ten African countries.

Interesting Facts For Smart Kids
With Curious Minds

Question 71

What does the "nature vs. nurture" debate in psychology refer to?

a) The influence of genetics versus environment on human development and behavior

b) The role of conscious versus unconscious processes in decision making

c) The impact of individual differences in personality traits

d) The importance of cognitive processes versus behavioral responses in learning

Answer 71

The "nature vs. nurture" debate refers to the longstanding question of how much of human behavior and development is influenced by genetic factors (nature) versus environmental factors (nurture). The nature perspective argues that genetic factors play a predominant role in determining traits and behaviors, meaning that people are born that way. On the other hand, nurture emphasizes the impact of environmental factors on human development, meaning that individuals are shaped by their experiences, social interactions, cultural influences, and upbringing.

Interesting Facts For Smart Kids
With Curious Minds

Question 72

Kshamavani celebrates the most important virtue in Jainism. What is it?

a) Truthfulness

b) Prayer

c) Forgiveness

d) Faith

Answer 72

Kshamavani, also known as "Forgiveness Day," is one of the most important dates in Jainism. Jainism, the largest religion in India, believes that this is the day to confess all misdeeds and forgive others for their mistakes. When asking for forgiveness, they use the phrase "Micchami Dukkadam," which roughly translates to "may all the evil that has been done become fruitless."

Interesting Facts For Smart Kids
With Curious Minds

Question 73

Who is the Catholic saint who was believed to have killed a dragon in the Middle Ages?

a) Saint George

b) Saint Paul

c) Cicero

d) Saint Thomas More

Answer 73

The crusaders told the legend of a knight who slayed a dragon: Saint George. The beast burned the crops, scared the villagers, and took young people as a sacrifice. Once, George was passing by when the dragon took the king's daughter. George took his sword and killed the beast.

Interesting Facts For Smart Kids
With Curious Minds

Question 74

In which English museum can music lovers see replicas of Mathew Street, Abbey Road Studios, and The Cavern, all iconic locations in the history of The Beatles?

a) The Beatles Story

b) Abbey Road

c) Prince of Wales Theater

d) Marylebone Station

Answer 74

Located in the band's hometown of Liverpool, The Beatles Story has memorabilia like John Lennon's famous round glasses and Ringo Starr's drum kit. The multimedia guides are available in twelve languages (English, French, Spanish, German, Italian, Russian, Polish, Mandarin, Cantonese, Japanese, Brazilian Portuguese, and Korean), proof that The Beatles had a universal appeal.

Interesting Facts For Smart Kids
With Curious Minds

Question 75

The tiniest vertebrate in the world is part of which animal species?

a) Frog

b) Lizard

c) Ant

d) Cockroach

David W. Leon
Fun Facts Books

Answer 75

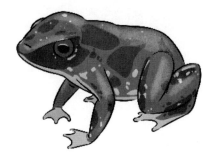

The animal with the tiniest backbone is likely the Paedophryne amauensis, a frog species from Papua New Guinea. It is considered the world's smallest vertebrate, measuring only about 7.7 millimeters (0.30 inches) in length.

Interesting Facts For Smart Kids
With Curious Minds

Question 76

What American holiday is usually celebrated with fireworks and hot dogs?

a) Mother's Day

b) Independence Day

c) Christmas Eve

d) Thanksgiving

David W. Leon
Fun Facts Books

Answer 76

The tradition of celebrating Independence Day with firework displays began in Philadelphia on July 4, 1777. Picnics and cookouts are popular on this day and usually feature hamburgers and hot dogs.

Interesting Facts For Smart Kids
With Curious Minds

Question 77

In the 15th century, a new philosophical approach spread a new set of values across Europe. What was that philosophical stance?

a) Stoicism

b) Romanticism

c) Humanism

d) Epicureanism

David W. Leon
Fun Facts Books

Answer 77

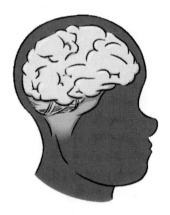

In the 15th century, Humanism, represented by Erasmus of Rotterdam and Thomas More, brought a new conception of human beings, knowledge, and philosophy. This approach originated with the Renaissance and retrieved the ideas and artistic expressions of the Classical period.

Interesting Facts For Smart Kids
With Curious Minds

Question 78

Who sculpted "David," one of the most famous statues in Florence, Italy?

a) Donatello

b) Michelangelo

c) Henry Moore

d) Auguste Rodin

David W. Leon
Fun Facts Books

Answer 78

Originally created for the Cathedral of Florence, Michelangelo sculpted David when he was only twenty-six years old. Michelangelo depicted King David as a confident young man standing nude. While most sculptors chose to portray David as victorious after slaying the giant Goliath, Michelangelo's famous work portrays David as he readied for battle.

Interesting Facts For Smart Kids
With Curious Minds

Question 79

How many chambers does a human heart have?

a) Five

b) Eight

c) Six

d) Four

Answer 79

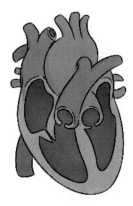

The aortic valve, mitral valve, pulmonary valve, and tricuspid valve are the names of the four chambers of the human heart. To pump blood through the body, the four valves open and close, which produces the sounds of a heartbeat.

Interesting Facts For Smart Kids
With Curious Minds

Question 80

While Black Friday marks the kickoff of shopping at brick and mortar stores, what day kicks off online Christmas shopping?

a) Giving Tuesday

b) Grey Thursday

c) Blue Wednesday

d) Cyber Monday

Answer 80

Coined by the online marketplace shop.org in 2005, Cyber Monday is now recognized as the day that online Christmas shopping begins. Just like Black Friday, online stores offer special sales and deals to entice customers to buy presents online.

Level 5
Voyage Into The Unexplored

Questions 81-100

We've Covered Science, History, Holidays, And Traveled The World. I Hope You've Discovered Some New Things To Learn About Further!

Interesting Facts For Smart Kids
With Curious Minds

Question 81

Which of the following artistic trends didn't develop in the 20th century?

a) Impressionism

b) Cubism

c) Futurism

d) Dadaismo

Answer 81

Impressionism developed in the 19th century. Some of the Impressionist names that stand out are Monet, Renoir, and Manet. Impressionist painters didn't try to paint reality as it is but as they saw it. They left aside the traditional three-dimensional approach to represent the world with unfinished shapes.

Interesting Facts For Smart Kids
With Curious Minds

Question 82

What Washington D.C. monument is the first to honor a man of color?

a) Jefferson Memorial

b) Martin Luther King Jr Memorial

c) Lincoln Memorial

d) National Mall

Answer 82

Featuring a 30-foot statue in the likeness of the civil rights leader, the Martin Luther King Jr Memorial shows him emerging from two boulders called "The Mountain of Despair." His likeness is carved into a stone called "The Stone of Hope." The monument is reflective of the lines "Out of the mountain of despair, a stone of hope," from his iconic "I Have a Dream" speech.

Interesting Facts For Smart Kids
With Curious Minds

Question 83

What is the world's largest single-celled organism?

a) Octopus

b) Killer Algae

c) Eels

d) Coral

David W. Leon
Fun Facts Books

Answer 83

The Aquarium Strain of Caulerpa taxifolia, often called "Killer Algae," is the largest single-celled organism in the world. It is called killer algae because it is highly invasive and destroys other native plants and fish habitats.

Interesting Facts For Smart Kids
With Curious Minds

Question 84

What infamous date is now called Pearl Harbor Remembrance Day?

a) November 12th

b) January 17th

c) December 7th

d) April 20th

David W. Leon
Fun Facts Books

Answer 84

President Franklin D. Roosevelt declared that December 7, 1941, would be "a date which will live in infamy" after Japan attacked the United States at Pearl Harbor. This event prompted the United States to join World War II. Each year, all flags are flown at half-mast to honor the 2300 Americans who died during the surprise attack.

Interesting Facts For Smart Kids
With Curious Minds

Question 85

Where was the first soccer World Cup played?

a) England

b) Uruguay

c) Italy

d) Brazil

Answer 85

Soccer's first world championship was played in 1930 in Uruguay. The host country won the trophy. There were two previous soccer competitions considered to be as important as the World Cup: the Olympic Games of 1924 and 1928, also won by Uruguay.

Interesting Facts For Smart Kids
With Curious Minds

Question 86

What is the name of the cemetery where musician Glen Miller, actor Lee Marvin, and politician Robert F. Kennedy are buried?

a) Arlington National Cemetery

b) Bonaventure Cemetery

c) Cave Hill Cemetery

d) Granary Burying Ground

Answer 86

These famous men, as well as 400,000 veterans, are buried in Washington D.C.'s Arlington Cemetery. John F. Kennedy and William H. Taft are the only two U.S. presidents buried in the national cemetery.

Interesting Facts For Smart Kids
With Curious Minds

Question 87

How many stars make up the Big Dipper?

a) Five

b) Three

c) Seven

d) Ten

Answer 87

The Big Dipper, which is part of the constellation Ursa Major (the Great Bear) is made up of seven bright stars. The seven stars that form the Big Dipper are: Alkaid (Eta Ursae Majoris), Mizar (Zeta Ursae Majoris), Alioth (Epsilon Ursae Majoris), Megrez (Delta Ursae Majoris), Phecda (Gamma Ursae Majoris), Dubhe (Alpha Ursae Majoris), and Merak (Beta Ursae Majoris).

Interesting Facts For Smart Kids
With Curious Minds

Question 88

What do people in Greece decorate for Christmas instead of trees?

a) Boats

b) Cars

c) Planes

d) Trains

Answer 88

The Greek tradition of "Karavaki," the decorating of boats instead of trees, stems from the close connection Greece has with the ocean. Saint Nicholas is also the patron saint of sailors, so it is also a way for Greeks to thank him for protecting their loved ones away at sea.

Interesting Facts For Smart Kids
With Curious Minds

Question 89

How long did the first airplane flight last?

a) A bit more than 10 seconds

b) 10 minutes

c) Half an hour

d) Two hours

Answer 89

The first successful airplane flight with a pilot on board lasted 12 seconds and covered 120 feet in December 1903. It was a biplane designed and built by the Wright brothers, and one of them was the pilot for that memorable short trip.

Interesting Facts For Smart Kids
With Curious Minds

Question 90

What is the name of the tomb/temple in Ireland that is older than both the Egyptian pyramids and England's Stonehenge?

a) Rock of Cashel

b) Benbulben

c) Dun Briste

d) Newgrange

David W. Leon
Fun Facts Books

Answer 90

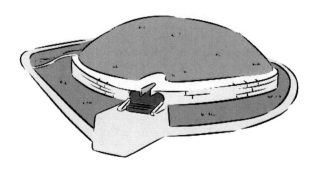

Located in the Boyne Valley, County Meath, Ireland, Newgrange is a circular mound with passageways and chambers inside. Built during the Stone Age, the passage and chambers align with the rising sun on the Winter Solstice.

Interesting Facts For Smart Kids
With Curious Minds

Question 91

What body part of an average human being is as long as their thumb?

a) Big toe

b) Spleen

c) Nose

d) Incisors

Answer 91

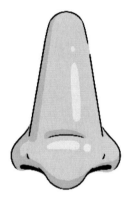

The body part that is commonly said to be as long as the thumb is the average adult's nose. The saying "as long as your thumb" is often used as a rough estimate or comparison for the length or size of something, but it's important to note that the actual length of a person's thumb or nose can vary significantly from individual to individual.

Interesting Facts For Smart Kids
With Curious Minds

Question 92

Known as the "Yule Lads," how many Father Christmases are recognized in Iceland?

a) Five

b) Thirteen

c) One

d) Twenty

Answer 92

For thirteen nights, children in Iceland leave out their shoes for each of the thirteen Yule Lads to either fill with candy (for good children) or rotting potatoes (for bad children). The Yule Lads all have funny names such as Spoon Licker (he licks spoons), Sausage Swiper (he steals sausages), and Candle Beggar (he steals candles).

Interesting Facts For Smart Kids
With Curious Minds

Question 93

Where did women first achieve the right to vote?

a) England

b) France

c) The US

d) New Zealand

Answer 93

Women's suffrage was implemented in some European countries and some states of the US during the 19th century. However, New Zealand was the first country to guarantee the right for every adult woman to vote in its constitution in 1893.

Interesting Facts For Smart Kids
With Curious Minds

Question 94

What is the name of the largest fortress in Europe?

a) Kremlin

b) Malbork Castle

c) Dover Castle

d) Prague Castle

Answer 94

Once the ultimate symbol of Soviet control, the Kremlin was built during the Middle Ages and is the largest fortress in Europe. The structure is famous for its red walls, but originally, they were painted white.

Interesting Facts For Smart Kids
With Curious Minds

Question 95

Why do ladybugs have spots?

a) To keep predators from eating them

b) To attract mates

c) Protection from sunlight

d) For good luck

Answer 95

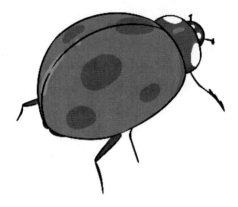

The bright coloration of ladybugs serves as a warning signal to potential predators. Ladybugs contain toxins in their bodies, which they obtain from their diet of plants and insects. The vivid colors and contrasting spots act as a visual warning to predators that they don't taste good.

Interesting Facts For Smart Kids
With Curious Minds

Question 96

What custom known as "Simbang Gabi" is a Christmas tradition in the Philippines?

a) Gift Giving

b) Evening Mass

c) Cooking Food

d) Volunteering

Answer 96

From December 16th-24th, a series of nine evening or night masses are held to prepare for Christmas Day. Known as Simbang Gabi, this tradition is observed by Filipino communities all over the world.

Interesting Facts For Smart Kids
With Curious Minds

Question 97

What was Enron?

a) A soccer team

b) An energy company

c) A global bank

d) A TV show

Answer 97

Enron Corporation was an important energy company in the US that collapsed in 2001 and shook Wall Street. It declared bankruptcy, affecting thousands of employees. It was a global scandal since the CEO had hidden multimillion dollar debts that eventually caused Enron to fall.

Interesting Facts For Smart Kids
With Curious Minds

Question 98

To which Irish city would you travel to visit the Guinness Storehouse?

a) Derry

b) Dublin

c) Limerick

d) Cork

Answer 98

Located in St. James Gate in Dublin, Ireland, the Guinness Storehouse celebrates Ireland's most famous alcohol export. While learning about how Guinness is made, visitors can also get a 360-degree view of Dublin from one of the city's highest vantage points.

Interesting Facts For Smart Kids
With Curious Minds

Question 99

What are the bumps on the top of your tongue called?

a) Papillae

b) Apex

c) Dorsum

d) Sulcus

Answer 99

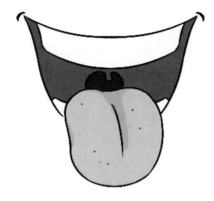

The bumps on the top surface of the tongue are called papillae (singular: papilla). Papillae are small structures that give the tongue its textured appearance. There are four different types of papillae that help the taste buds to detect and transmit signals of taste to the brain, allowing us to perceive different flavors.

Interesting Facts For Smart Kids
With Curious Minds

Question 100

What does Ded Moroz, a Soviet version of Santa Clause, use to pull his troika (sleigh) instead of reindeer?

a) Sled Dogs

b) Cows

c) Horses

d) Cats

Answer 100

Instead of eight reindeer, Ded Moroz's troika is pulled by three horses and delivers gifts on New Year's Eve rather than Christmas. He carries a staff, can appear in a red or blue costume, and resides not at the North Pole, but at his estate in the town of Veliky Ustyug in Russia. These changes were made during the Soviet period in Russia to create a more secular holiday celebration.

Thank You & Leave A Review

Have you ever tried something scary and new, and it seems the odds are against you? If yes, then you likely know exactly how my wife and I feel right now.

We're taking a leap and trying our hand at writing and sharing our favorite family tradition of trivia night.

Our goal is to create high quality books for everyone to enjoy and hopefully learn a few new things too.

Your feedback will help us to keep writing these books and it would mean a lot to hear from you.

Posting a review is the best and easiest way to support the work of independent authors like us. If you've enjoyed any of our books so far and have 2 minutes to spare, we would be so thankful!

We truly appreciate all your love and support!

Open the camera app on your phone
Hold phone so the QR Code appears in view
Tap the pop-up link for the QR Code

Your Free Gift

Grab your FREE Gifts:

BONUS 1: Our best-selling e-book

BONUS 2: An exclusive, never-before-seen, e-book with an additional 100 interesting and fun facts!

Open the camera app on your phone
Hold phone so the QR Code appears in view
Tap the pop-up link for the QR Code

Check Out The Full Series

Enjoyed the book?
Check out the full series!

Open the camera app on your phone
Hold phone so the QR Code appears in view
Tap the pop-up link for the QR Code

Made in United States
North Haven, CT
06 December 2024

61891420R00136